To Jane, Milena, Amelia & Harris, who kindly feed our little cat
 when we're away —A.McQ.

To Rosie, with love from Rosi — R.B.

Lulu does a great job of finding out
how to care for cats and how to be
responsible before she gets her little cat.

If you would like to find out more about how to look after your cat or
what to think about when adopting a cat, the National Cats Adoption
Cenre is a great place to get information: www.cats.org.uk/learn

First published in the UK in 2017 by
Alanna Books
46 Chalvey Road East,
Slough, Berkshire, SL1 2LR

www.alannabooks.com

ISBN: 978-1-907825-163
Printed and bound in China

Lulu Gets a Cat!

Anna McQuinn
Illustrated by Rosalind Beardshaw

ALANNA BOOKS

Lulu loves cats.
She wants a real one.

Mummy says looking after a cat
is a lot of work.

Lulu decides to find out more.

She learns that cats are super
at smelling and hearing.

Lulu reads all about how to care for cats. She pretends Dinah is a real cat and practices looking after her.

At last Mummy agrees. Lulu can get a cat!
Mummy and Lulu find out how to adopt one.

At the cat shelter, they meet Jeremy.
He shows them three perfect cats.

Before Lulu can decide, one little cat chooses her!

Jeremy says moving is scary for cats.
He gives Lulu a list of things that will help.

Lulu will be back as soon as
everything at home is ready.

All the next day, Lulu and Mummy shop.
What a lot of stuff for a little cat!

Lulu and Daddy make a special corner where her cat will settle in.

Finally Lulu is ready to bring her cat home.

But the little cat is afraid.
Her own blanket makes
her feel safe.

Lulu tells her not to worry.

At home, the little cat stays in the carry case. After a while, she comes out and sniffs around.

Lulu watches for now. She knows
her cat isn't ready to play just yet.

Lulu decides to call her cat *Makeda*.
It is the name of an African Queen.

Lulu takes excellent care of Makeda.
She feeds her and gives her fresh water.

One day, Lulu's friend Tayo brings
a special present for Makeda.

Tayo and Lulu play with Makeda
all afternoon.

At last Makeda feels right at home.
Her favourite thing is to snuggle Lulu!

Every evening Lulu reads to Makeda.
Tonight's story is about a famous cat.

Lulu loves her new little cat. And bed-time stories with Makeda are the best of all.